When the Snake bites the Sun

AN ABORIGINAL STORY
Told by David Mowaljarlai
Compiled by Pamela Lofts

SCHOLASTIC
SYDNEY AUCKLAND NEW YORK TORONTO LONDON MEXICO CITY
NEW DELHI HONG KONG BUENOS AIRES PUERTO RICO

Long, long ago, in the East,
behind the world,
there lived two suns.
A big fat mother sun
and a little daughter sun.

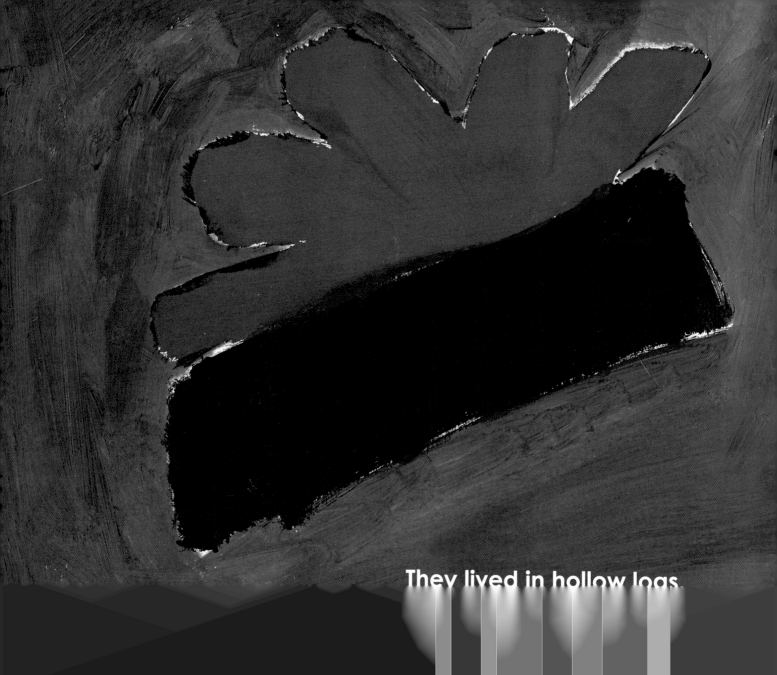

They lived in hollow logs.

They came out
to give the world light,
but they shone so fiercely
and for so long
that everything began to burn up.

The ground became scorched.
The rivers dried up . . .

The animals began to die of thirst.

The mother sun, by this time, had got so fat, that she could no longer squeeze out of her log.

So, she sent her daughter out alone.

The little sun rolled across the sea
to Marungi Biddi Biddi – an island
where two men lived.

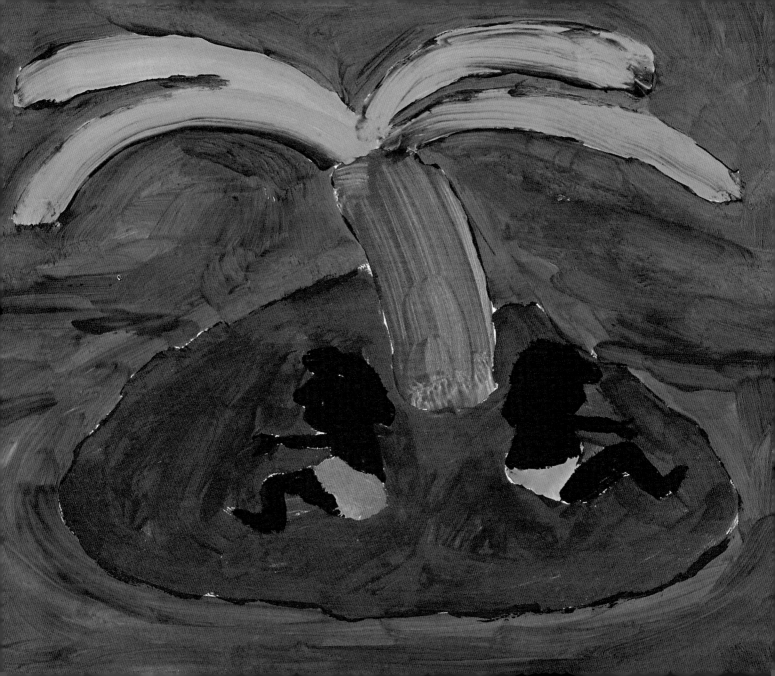

One was a good man, who had always
looked after the two suns.
The other was a bad man.

The bad man chased the little sun,
and poked her with his spear.

She was afraid he would kill her and leave the world in darkness.

So she took off into space to escape him,

getting hotter and hotter

as she climbed.

But up there in the sky, high above the earth,
lived a snake.
Suddenly, he rushed at her . . .

and bit her.

Now she could go no higher.
And, getting weaker and cooler,
she rolled away down towards the
edge of the earth.

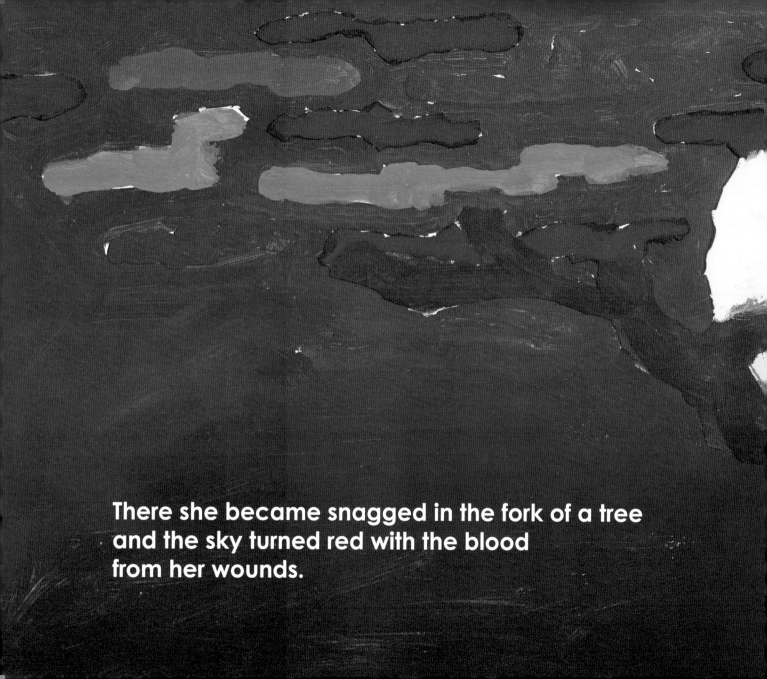

There she became snagged in the fork of a tree
and the sky turned red with the blood
from her wounds.

At last, she slipped down
into the mists below.
And the world became dark.

She went back to her mother,
who looked after her
till she was strong again.

Ever since that time, the little sun has made
her journey from the east to the west to give
the world day and night.

There must always be a day for light and heat . . .

followed by the darkness of night
for the world to cool and rest –
so that it will never burn up again.